Something Truly Dreadful

Matthew Salinas

Coalescence Publishing, LLC

Contents

O n October 13th, Wes Andrews and his friends set out to explore the local, rundown haunted house. Despite it being geared toward children, they figured that, with nothing better to do, it might be fun to heckle the low-budget attraction. But after that night, no one ever saw or heard from them again. The haunted house itself vanished without a trace, taking Wes, his friends, and a significant portion of their town with it.

All that remained at the scene of their disappearance were scattered Polaroid photos, a shattered camera, and unsettling traces—teeth, strands of hair, and fragments of bone.

The events that followed unfolded over seven chilling hours...

Chapter One

October 13th, 2001 - 5:00 PM

*T*he following is a transcript of the AOL Instant Messenger conversation between Wes Andrews and his friends: Veronica Whitney, Charlie Moore, Louise Katin, and Sydney Wuller. The conversation takes place from 5:00 PM to 5:20 PM.

BandicootTheCrash: This town sucks.

VeR0N1Ca: Tell me about it...

WesAndDrew: Well, I heard there's some new "attraction" in town.

Thelma?NoLouise: Please don't tell me it's what I'm thinking of...

SkindKnees22: I'm so worn out, guys. The skate park was packed today. Spent half my time fighting dudes off with my board. Just wanna chill tonight lol.

BandicootTheCrash: Humble brag, much?

SkindKnees22: Maybe. Jealous much, Charlie?

BandicootTheCrash: Screw you lol

VeR0N1Ca: Weren't we supposed to be figuring out what to do tonight? It's Saturday, and the fact that we're all sitting here messaging each other... it's kinda lame and depressing.

Thelma?NoLouise: Well, if Wes is suggesting what I think he is, it might be about to get even more lame and depressing.

WesAndDrew: C'mon, it can't be that bad. Besides, Louise, when have we ever turned down a solid chance to talk shit about something?

VeR0N1Ca: That's so true lmao

BandicootTheCrash: I'm in, I got nothing else going on. But, uh, what the hell are we even talking about?

Thelma?NoLouise: Are you telling him, or am I, Wes?

SkindKnees22: Telling us *what*?

WesAndDrew: That haunted house that opened last weekend. It's supposedly for little kids, but everyone's been talking trash about it. I doubt it's scary, but it'll be hilarious to heckle it as we go through.

BandicootTheCrash: Idk... you guys expect me to spend my hard-earned allowance on some kiddie haunted house?

WesAndDrew: It's literally a dollar.

BandicootTheCrash: Oh, fine lol. It can't be worse than that lame carnival the church puts on every year.

SkindKnees22: Yeah, the rides suck, but I keep going back for that sweet, sweet cotton candy lol.

VeR0N1Ca: So, are we all meeting there?

WesAndDrew: Unless someone has a better idea?

VeR0N1Ca: You guys know my parents don't let me go out at night without an "escort" lol.

SkindKnees22: I'm riding over, so unless you want to take that lame scooter of yours...

VeR0N1Ca: Hey, asshat! It's a *Razor*! Everyone had one. It's been collecting dust in my garage.

Thelma?NoLouise: Ooo, someone's getting defensive lol. JK, JK. But I can be your +1 ;) I'll swing by and pick you up.

BandicootTheCrash: Yo, Wes. You're dropping off my CDs before we head over, right?

WesAndDrew: Yeah, yeah. I didn't get through all of them, though. You gave me, like, five days, man.

BandicootTheCrash: Dude, if my older brother knew I lent you *any* of his CDs, he'd kill me. Consider yourself lucky.

WesAndDrew: Yeah, yeah...

VeR0N1Ca: So, where is this place anyway?

Thelma?NoLouise: Rankine Road, by the old elementary school. The flyers are plastered all over town.

SkindKnees22: I'll see you guys there around 6, I take it? You lame-asses are always late anyway.

BandicootTheCrash: Not everyone's a freak about punctuality, Sydney. Get a life.

SkindKnees22: Screw you, dickhead.

WesAndDrew: I'll see everyone there. I'm telling you, it can't be worse than staying in tonight, right?

SkindKnees22: Don't be too late, losers lol

(SkindKnees22 has signed off)

BandicootTheCrash: Don't forget those CDs, Wes!!!

(BandicootTheCrash has signed off)

VeR0N1Ca: I'll be waiting, Louise. Just don't take forever.

Thelma?NoLouise: Aye aye, captain.

(Thelma?NoLouise has signed off)

VeR0N1Ca: This better not suck, Wes.

WesAndDrew: I promise it won't.

(VeR0N1Ca has signed off)

(WesAndDrew has signed off)

***

Wes pushed his chair back from the family desktop computer in the hallway and headed downstairs into the kitchen.

"Hey Mom, I'm going out with my friends tonight!"

"Don't be out past curfew!" his mother called back.

"Swear to God, Wes," his father added, "one more complaint from Mrs. Neomi about you fucking with her porch decorations..."

Wes crossed his fingers behind his back, even though neither of his parents could see him from the family room. "Yeah, yeah. I learned my lesson, I swear!"

Then a thought struck him. "Hey, Mom, do you know where that old Polaroid camera is? I want to take some group photos tonight."

"Should be in the front hallway closet on the top rack, with all your sports crap."

"Thanks!" Wes finished tying his shoes, then opened the front hallway closet and grabbed the camera. *Tonight is going to be entertaining,* he thought as he reached for the door. "Don't wait up!"

A wide smile spread across his face as he set off, camera in hand, toward Charlie's house.

It was the last time Mr. and Mrs. Andrews would see their son.

Photograph Details:

- **Date:** October 13th, 2001

- **Time:** Approximately 5:28 PM

- **Photographer:** Wes Andrews, age 15

- **Subject:** Family front yard tree, left of driveway, planted ten years prior

Description of Last Known Appearance:

Wes Andrews was last seen wearing a denim jacket, blue jeans, and a black graphic T-shirt. He stands approximately 5'10", weighs between 160-170 lbs, and has brown hair, brown eyes, and a clean-shaven face.

This was the only photograph Wes took that evening.

Chapter Two

October 13th, 2001 - 6:00 PM, Missing Subjects Arrive at "Doug's Den of Insanity"

B *ased on collected text records and eyewitness reports, Sydney Wuller was the first to arrive. The following is a dramatized portrayal of events believed to have occurred before the "haunted house" incident.*

Sydney arrived first, as usual, and spent a few minutes skating around the parking lot. *I don't get how they walk everywhere. It's so boring.* She circled the lot, her mind wandering back to Charlie. *I know he likes me, but I don't think he'll ever do anything about it. Way too insecure to make the first move. Am I going to have to?*

Lost in thought, she didn't notice Louise and Veronica sneaking up behind her.

"Boo!" they shouted in unison.

Sydney whipped around, swinging her board reflexively, narrowly missing both of them. "Holy shit! Don't do that!"

Louise ducked, laughing. "Whoa there, killer!"

Veronica held up her hands, wide-eyed. "We didn't mean to scare you *that* much, Syd!"

Sydney let out a breath, shaking her head. "Sorry, but if you sneak up on a girl at night in an empty parking lot, expect her to be ready to defend herself."

Louise straightened, brushing hair out of her face. "Fair enough."

Veronica glanced at her wristwatch, tapping her foot impatiently. *I can't believe my parents won't just give me a phone. If I'm out past curfew, they could just call me...* "So, the boys are late as usual?"

"It's only been a few minutes." Sydney scratched her head.

"It's 6:05, Syd," Louise remarked, looking around.

"Actually, 6:08," Veronica corrected, frowning at her watch, still lost in her thoughts about her parents and their outdated curfew rules. *One day, they'll realize I'm practically an adult, and a cell phone is, like, a necessity.*

Sydney squinted. "Wait—are those dork-wads one and two on the horizon?"

"Dorks, ho!" Louise pointed and laughed as Wes and Charlie ambled toward them, clearly in no rush.

Charlie leaned over to Wes, blushing furiously. "You think she knows I like her?"

Wes sighed. "Dude, everyone knows you like Sydney. It's beyond obvious."

Charlie groaned. "That bad, huh?"

"Like, terminally bad, dude," Wes assured him.

"Well, shit..." Charlie muttered, eyes glued to the ground as they approached the girls. *Don't do anything dumb, and don't say anything stupid. C'mon, man, you've got this.*

"Hey, boys! Took you long enough," Veronica called across the empty lot.

Charlie raised an eyebrow. "Looking this good takes time, ladies." *Crap! What did I just tell you?*

Wes burst out laughing. "Yeah, Casanova here spent, like, ten minutes fixing that bird's nest he calls hair."

The girls all laughed, and Charlie turned red enough to look sunburned.

Veronica put her hands on her hips. "So, what's the deal with this place, Wes? It looks like the kind of place homeless people go to feel better about being homeless."

Wes grinned. "I think it's officially called Doug's Den of Insanity or some hokey name like that."

"Yeah, ages seven to twelve, I think the flyers said," Louise added.

Sydney feigned a shudder. "Oh no, how terrifying! I hope we don't have nightmares!"

"Cool it, Syd," Wes chuckled. "Like I said, it'll be fun to make fun of. Might as well check it out before it goes out of business. Who knows? Maybe we'll get at least one decent jump scare."

Charlie, having regained his normal pale color, chimed in, "I mean, for a buck, it'll at least be a story to tell people on Monday."

Louise nodded, smiling. "Exactly."

Veronica tapped her foot on the pavement. "Are we gonna stand here and talk about how crappy this place looks, or are we going in? I don't have all night."

Louise stretched and cracked her neck. "Ready to rock when you are, fellas."

"Step right up!" an unfamiliar voice boomed from across the lot.

All five turned and stared.

"No need to be shy! Come on by and check out Doug's Den of Insanity! Hosted by yours truly... Doug!" The voice beckoned, oddly cheerful.

Wes smirked. "Guess he means us."

They walked over to a small wooden hovel, barely big enough for the man standing inside. It looked to be about three feet wide and six feet tall, yet somehow it accommodated the grinning man who eagerly awaited them.

"Why, hello!" Doug greeted them with a toothy smile. "I must say, we usually only get the little ones here, given the reputation of this place, but I'm delighted to see it looks like we're... branching out." He chuckled to himself, his laughter unnervingly high-pitched, as if there were some hidden joke only he understood.

"Yeah, um, thanks, Doug," Veronica finally broke the silence. "I heard it's only a dollar?"

Doug raised an index finger. "Indeed, indeed! Such a small price for such an *incredible* experience."

"What exactly is the 'incredible experience'?" Louise asked, curiosity piqued.

"Ah, yes, eh hm," Doug cleared his throat theatrically. "Three terrifying rooms. Each is more diabolical than the last. You have three hours to make your way through and come out on the other side. But be warned, not all make it through. And those who don't..." His voice trailed off ominously.

"Go on..." Wes leaned in, as intrigued as the rest of them.

"Meet with a *horrible fate*! Muahahaha!" Doug's laugh became more deranged as he pressed a button on a small sound machine, releasing a crack of thunder sound effect and strobing lights imitating flashes of lightning.

"You know," Charlie chuckled, "I gotta say, this guy is pretty damn convincing." He laughed. "Your commitment to the bit—kudos, man."

"Aww, thank you, young man." Doug bowed slightly. "I've been working on the spiel since we opened last week. I think I've finally nailed it."

The group clapped, amused but slightly unsettled. Despite the rundown look of the place and the fact that it was just a small shack decorated with Halloween props, there was an uneasy tension in the air. Doug had an aura about him—something menacing that made the hairs on the backs of their necks prickle. He held their gaze in silence just a bit too long, enough to send a ripple of discomfort through each of them.

"I have just three requests before you attempt to brave this Den of Insanity," Doug said, eyes gleaming as he took in their nervous smirks.

"Well, what are they?" Sydney asked.

Doug turned his palms up, speaking with dramatic emphasis. "First and foremost—have fun, and tell your friends about this place. We need people to spread the word. Business isn't as booming as I'd hoped, especially so close to Halloween." He looked slightly sheepish before continuing. "Second, here." He handed each of them a small piece of paper and a pencil. "If you don't mind, write down two or more things you find *absolutely terrifying*. I'm always looking for ideas, and next year, I'd like to ramp things up with some fresh scares. You can hand them to the ticket taker over there," he pointed to the building entrance, where a man with a shaggy haircut stood motion-less, eyes fixed somewhere far away.

"Third, and most importantly—no flash photography." He point-ed at the Polaroid camera hanging around Wes's neck. "Sorry, but it's a safety risk. If you'd like, I can take a group photo of you now and again after you come out." He leaned in, lowering his voice. "Besides, I wouldn't want you spilling the beans on what's inside and ruining the fun."

Wes frowned slightly, gripping the camera.

"Not saying you would, good sir," Doug raised his hands in mock surrender. "I just don't want to risk it, is all."

The group exchanged looks before Wes shrugged. "Yeah, I suppose that's fair," he said, handing over the camera.

"Thanks, big guy! Now, everyone get together," Doug directed, motioning them into position.

The group huddled shoulder to shoulder.

"Smile! 3, 2, 1... perfect." Doug snapped the photo and carefully placed it under a coffee mug in his booth. "Now you'll have a before photo. It'll be cool to compare to the after one. You know, once you're all insane!" He cackled loudly. He hit the button again.

Veronica rolled her eyes, letting out a loud, audible sigh as she extended a fist with a crumpled dollar bill toward him. "Here."

Doug grinned wide. "Thank you, miss. Everyone, step on up!"

They each fished out a dollar, handing them over in turn.

"Excellent! Well, see you all on the other side!" Doug yanked the booth curtain closed with dramatic flair.

"I have to say, Wes," Sydney said, smirking. "That alone was worth a dollar."

They all laughed, making their way over to the ticket taker.

"So, what did you guys put down?" Louise asked, glancing around.

"I'm not telling you anything," Charlie muttered, folding his slip of paper.

"Ooo, someone's embarrassed," Sydney teased as Charlie flushed red.

"I think we can talk about it after," Wes said, grinning. "It'll give us something to laugh about on the way home." *Man, I really hope Doug doesn't break that camera or my ass is grass.*

"I'm not afraid of anything," Veronica scoffed. "This is all so childish."

"Sure you're not," Louise replied with a smirk. *She's probably afraid of something stupid like snakes or spiders.*

The ticket taker greeted them in a long, drawn-out tone with a strange emphasis on the 's'. "Welcome, boys and girls. I'll take those," he said, extending his hand for their slips of paper. He collected each one, folding them neatly.

"Due to limited space, I can only let you in groups of two, with about fifteen minutes between each pair," he continued. "And I must emphasize—no waiting for others to catch up and absolutely no going backward. Each group will have a separate timer, and you'll have three hours to reach the other side, as I'm sure you heard from Doug."

"Well... great," Wes muttered. "Guess we're splitting up?"

"I call Veronica!" Louise shouted, pulling her friend close.

Veronica grinned. "That's fine with me."

"I guess that leaves you and me?" Sydney looked at Charlie, a slight smile playing on her lips.

Oh man, just say yes. Don't mess this up. She's definitely making a move.

Wes pulled Charlie in close. "Go with her, man. I'll be fine on my own."

"Seriously?" Charlie's eyes widened.

"Just go, dude!" Wes gave him a firm shove, and Charlie staggered forward into Sydney.

"Yes, I... uh... think we'd make a good team," Charlie half-smiled, half-grimaced at how cringe he sounded.

Sydney raised an eyebrow, looking him up and down. "Whatever."

"I'll go last on my own," Wes said, shrugging. "It was my idea anyway, so no big deal."

"Alright then, it's decided." The ticket taker pointed to Louise and Veronica. "You two are up. The rest of you will go in at fifteen-minute increments after they get started. Good luck!"

"See you guys in a few," Louise said, waving cheerfully.

"This better not suck too bad, Wes," Veronica muttered, giving him one last look before disappearing into the haunted house with Louise.

"Well, guess we just wait here," Wes said, watching the door swing shut behind them.

"So... scared?" Charlie asked, trying to sound casual.

"Nah," Sydney smirked, "it's not like any of it's real anyway."

- The only remaining trace of "Doug's Den of Insanity" was the ticket taker, identified as Stanley [Redacted], age 32, Caucasian male (pictured above). He currently resides in the Seymour Hospital for Mental Illness.

- Stanley has been unable to provide any explanation for the disappearances of the children and has been deemed mentally unfit to stand trial.

- All other information remains confidential due to the ongoing investigation.

Chapter Three

October 13th, 2001 - Louise and Veronica enter "Doug's Den of Insanity"

L *ouise Kitan and Veronica Whitney were the first two to enter the attraction. The following is a dramatic retelling of the events believed to have occurred based on photos and evidence found at the scene of their grisly murders.*

"So... this is kind of lame," Louise muttered, glancing around the dingy haunted house. Cardboard cutouts of monsters, zombies, and vampires cluttered the first room, accompanied by poorly projected ghosts on thin sheets strung along a laundry line.

"Yeah... I didn't expect much from this place, especially after the glowing endorsement you and Wes gave it," Veronica laughed, kicking over a cardboard werewolf and watching it flop to the floor with a disappointing thud.

A fog machine hummed in the corner, pumping out a weak mist that barely filled the room. The setup looked like something a couple of teenagers might throw together for quick cash. As they moved through, faint howls and groans played from a hidden boombox. The whole experience felt half-hearted and utterly underwhelming.

"I can't imagine this scares kids either," Veronica snickered.

"Oh, Veronica, hold me!" Louise wrapped her arms around her from behind. "I don't think my delicate heart can take much more."

Veronica pushed her off, rolling her eyes. "That was honestly scarier than anything else in this room."

They laughed as they reached the end of the first room and pushed open the door to the next. Instantly, they were swallowed by darkness. The room was pitch black, offering no outlines or details. As they ventured inside, the door slammed shut behind them.

"Crap!" Louise yelped, jumping forward.

"Really? That's so cliché," Veronica said, though she'd instinctively inched closer to Louise, refusing to admit the door slam had startled her too.

"I bet they just have someone by the door to pop out and slam it shut," Louise mused. "Cheap but effective," she laughed.

"I guess..." Veronica replied, sighing.

"C'mon, you don't have to be so serious all the time, Veronica. It's just us here—no one's going to think you're any less cool for admitting something was kinda scary," Louise teased, nudging her. "Besides, I *totally* saw you jump."

Veronica shot her a look. "Whatever."

"You know, I have no idea where we're even going," Louise admitted after a beat.

"No kidding," Veronica muttered, squinting into the void. "This room is dark as hell, and there's zero indication of where anything is."

Louise grinned. "Don't tell me you're afraid of the dark."

Veronica's cheeks flushed as she thought of the slip of paper she'd handed over when they entered. *Isolation.* Pure darkness in an empty room wasn't far off—but at least here, she still had Louise. "S-shut up!"

Louise chuckled, placing a finger to her lips. "Your secret's safe with me, kiddo."

They pressed onward into the darkness. Despite its lack of theatrics, the room felt unsettling, as if it stretched on far longer than seemed possible.

"How much longer does this room go on?" Veronica's voice echoed strangely.

"No clue," Louise replied, squinting ahead.

Suddenly, a strobe light flickered to life, casting the room in harsh, fluorescent flashes. A small, albino man stood before them, arms raised.

Both girls screamed, and Veronica instinctively clung to Louise.

"Beware the third and final room!" he bellowed, his pale skin blending into the flashing light while his beady red eyes fixed on them. "For it only gets scarier from here on!"

"Oh man," Louise laughed, catching her breath. "That actually got me good."

Veronica, still recovering, muttered, "Jesus! How long have you been waiting here to do that?"

The man smirked. "They let me know when you enter the room. I watch on a monitor until you're near, then I come out, stand on this," he pointed to an "X" marked with electrical tape, "hit the floor button to strobe the lights, yell, and then... I get paid and go home."

"Well, that kinda ruins the mystery," Louise frowned.

"Whatever. Please proceed to the next room and prepare for more..." he took a dramatic breath, "*Insanity!*" He flailed his arms wildly.

"Sure thing, little man," Veronica muttered, pushing past him to open the door.

Louise leaned in, grinning. "She's just mad you scared her."

The albino man chuckled, giving her a knowing nod. "All in a day's work."

The two women exited the last room and found themselves in what looked like a miniature village. Cobblestone streets wound between small, thatched-roof huts with wide, open windows. Though better lit than the previous room, everything seemed bathed in an eerie, perpetual shadow.

"This is... highly unusual," Veronica murmured, tiptoeing slowly down the cobblestone path toward the village center.

Louise trailed behind, glancing into one of the windows—and froze.

"Everything alright?" Veronica asked, continuing a few more steps before noticing Louise had stopped at the village's edge, eyes fixed on something inside the hut.

"Hey, you okay, Lou?" Veronica's skin prickled with unease. *What is she looking at?* A wave of dread rolled through her as she cautiously stepped closer to Louise, wiping away the cold sweat on her brow. Her stomach clenched, and her mouth felt sour. She had never seen Louise so utterly petrified.

Reaching out, Veronica extended a hand, speaking softly. "Take my hand, Lou... come on."

Louise's gaze finally shifted to meet hers, and she shuddered. Veronica leaned in to look inside the window, desperate to understand what had paralyzed her friend. In the shadows of the hut, two small children stood, their empty, black eyes fixed unblinkingly on Louise.

"What the...?" Veronica mouthed.

One child was a preteen boy, the other a young girl, both dressed in strange, outdated clothing. Their eyes were dark voids, unblinking, and through the faint light streaming from the window, their petrified faces seemed to merge with the girls' reflections. Time stretched out painfully as none of them moved, and Veronica could hear Louise's shallow, rapid breaths.

"I don't think they're going to attack us," Veronica whispered, trying to steady her voice.

Louise swallowed, nodding slowly. "I know. They're... mannequins."

Veronica blinked, then let out a loud sigh. "Wait, what?" She glanced again and smacked her forehead. "They're mannequins, and you *knew*?"

"Get me out of here, Veronica." Louise's voice was a desperate whisper, her eyes wide and pleading.

"Wait a minute," Veronica smirked. "Are you... afraid of mannequins?"

Louise nodded vigorously, her eyes wide.

"I bet that's what you wrote on your scrap of paper, isn't it?" Veronica laughed.

Louise's expression grew more desperate. "Joke time later. Just help me."

Guilt washed over Veronica as she saw the genuine fear in her friend's eyes. "Alright, alright," she whispered. "Close your eyes and stick out your hand. I've got you."

Louise reluctantly shut her eyes, stretching her hand forward. *For the love of God, just get me out of here.* She felt Veronica's firm grip take her hand and guide her forward. They turned a few times, and before long, they reached the end of the room.

"You can open your eyes now, Lou," Veronica assured her, placing a comforting hand on her shoulder.

Louise opened her eyes to find herself in front of a door marked *Exit.*

"All in all, I gotta say, totally worth the dollar," Veronica smirked. *I can't believe she's terrified of mannequins.*

"Wooo, I think I might actually agree with you," Louise laughed, though the embarrassment lingered. *If she tells anyone about the mannequins, I swear I'll tell everyone she's afraid of the dark.*

Together, they pushed open the door, stepping out into a narrow, damp alleyway behind the building. A chill swept over them, a strange comfort after the manufactured scares they'd just endured. They couldn't help but feel a little silly for being so spooked by what was essentially a kids' haunted house. Then, across the alleyway, a light flickered on, casting an eerie glow over a brick wall directly opposite them.

"A... are you seeing this too?" Louise murmured.

"I'm afraid so," Veronica replied, her voice barely above a whisper.

Across the wall, in either red spray paint or something far more sinister, were the words *Save Yourself.* Surrounding it, equally haunting phrases sprawled in different handwritings: *Run! This is where you all die... The rooms are a lie. Doug has damned us all.* Some of the phrases were painted in the same alarming red, while others were scrawled in black or white, fading into the brickwork.

"Somehow, I get the feeling this part"—Louise gestured at the wall—"isn't meant for kids."

Veronica glanced around the alley, uneasy. "Yeah, I'm getting that vibe too, Lou."

The light above them began to flicker, and a sound like rushing water started to fill the air, growing louder by the second. As it intensified, they realized it wasn't water at all—it was screaming. Their eyes met, and without another word, they sprinted down the alleyway, the desperate cries echoing behind them.

The narrow, winding path led them to yet another door. With nowhere else to turn, they shoved it open and hurried inside, slamming it shut behind them.

Louise dropped to her knees, panting. "Dear God... what kind of haunted house lets you out in an alley like that?" She coughed, trying to catch her breath. "I mean, good grief, no wonder this place has been getting awful reviews." She looked around and took in the room's sparse furnishings, white sheets draped over random pieces of furniture. It looked like they'd stumbled into some sort of storage room or warehouse.

Veronica took a steadying breath, her mind racing. *It's fine. It's over. Just one last big scare.* "This is just cruel, plain and simple." She scanned the room, searching for an exit. "But... I don't think this is part of the haunted house, Lou."

They both looked around, and their expressions shifted from relief to confusion.

Louise looked to her side and saw nothing. She was utterly alone in the room, surrounded only by the dim light and the ghostly, sheet-covered shapes.

Veronica stood frozen, staring into the vast, empty room illuminated by a single, flickering light fixture above her. There was nothing else—no furnishings, no walls in sight—only an unsettling, hollow emptiness.

Both girls were completely and inexplicably alone.

This doesn't make any sense. I saw her come in here with me. Veronica's mind raced, frantically trying to make sense of how she'd ended up alone, separated from Louise.

I need to get back to the group. This is beyond creepy. Louise took one tentative step forward, then another, her resolve strengthening with each step. She had to find a way out. A slight gust of air blew into the room, ruffling one of the white sheets covering the scattered furnishings. *Oh hell no.* She squinted, her breath catching as she saw something beneath the sheet: feet—cold, lifeless, plastic feet, likely attached to an entire mannequin.

"What the fuck is up with all these mannequins?" she muttered, feeling the emptiness press in around her. Suddenly, a loud rustling behind her made her whirl around. "Who's there? Veronica?" Her voice echoed back, her only answer.

"If you're there, this isn't funny. I swear to God, I'll tell everyone you're afraid of the dark if you don't come out right now!"

Across the building, Veronica whispered into the vast emptiness of her room. "Louise?" Her voice trembled, and she took a deep breath. "I don't know where you are. Please, help me. I can't do this… by myself." As she inched forward, the dim light above grew brighter, pulling her toward it until she stood directly beneath it. *It's safe here,* she told herself, hoping that staying put would mean Louise would find her. *Just stay here. Louise will come.*

"Veronica?" Louise stammered, every hair on her neck standing on end as she felt eyes on her. *I'm not alone in here. Oh God, I'm not alone in here.* She spun around and screamed, face-to-face with a towering mannequin looming over her. Instinctively, she swung her fist, watching as it toppled over, its head rolling away into the darkness.

"Fuck me!" she gasped, her breath ragged. She ran trembling hands through her hair, trying to calm her nerves, but it was no use. She glanced around the room, realizing with horror that more and more of the white sheets were beginning to shift and ripple as if concealing something alive.

She took several steps back. "That can't be good."

Everything beneath the sheets began to shake violently. Without a second thought, Louise bolted toward the far end of the room, refusing to look back. Her only focus was the path ahead. A rundown door with an opaque glass pane loomed in the distance. *There it is. Get out. Find Veronica.* It was the only thought racing through her mind as she reached the door, her hands fumbling at the doorknob, desperate to escape.

The door refused to budge.

"Lou...ise..." a disembodied voice whispered, soft yet chilling, from just behind her shoulder.

"No... no, it's just my mind playing tricks," Louise muttered, pulling and pushing desperately at the door. It didn't give an inch.

"We... need... new... flesh..." The voice morphed, shifting between male and female, young and old, blending into a ghastly chorus, as if a crowd of voices spoke through a single mouth.

"This isn't real. Get a grip, Louise." Her voice trembled as she began pounding on the glass of the door, ready to break her way out if she had to.

"Why so scared, Louise? We promise it doesn't hurt... much..." The voices laughed, taunting her, closer now.

Unable to resist the pull, she turned—and instantly regretted it. The floor was covered with white sheets, which had fallen to reveal hundreds, if not thousands, of mannequins. All of them, now freed from their fabric restraints, lurched toward her, moving their arms and legs in a jerky, mechanical fashion, each movement unnatural and grotesque.

Louise pressed herself against the door, her eyes wide with terror. "Get away! Stay the fuck away from me! Veronica!"

"No Veronica," the voices replied, a sinister, unified whisper. "Only us, Louise."

She cowered against the door, shielding her eyes, her heart pounding as the smell of stale air filled her lungs. A crack sounded behind her as the glass shattered, and a cold, plastic hand reached through, gripping her face. Fingers pressed around her mouth, muffling her screams until darkness took over, and she slipped into unconsciousness.

"Louise?" Veronica murmured, sitting beneath the dim light, hands clasped in her lap. *She'll come for me. There's no way she wouldn't find me.* The thought brought her a fragile sense of comfort. Your friends will come for you. Louise will find you. It was the last thought she held on to as the light above flickered, then cut out, plunging her into absolute darkness.

• This photograph was recovered from the scene of the disappearances and is believed to capture the entrance to the "warehouse" area where the children were herded after exiting "Doug's Den of Insanity." Business records show the warehouse was purchased by Doug [Redacted] as storage for additional haunted house props.

- All that remained within the facility were fragments—bone, flesh, and strands of hair—from the five missing children. This photo was discovered in a carefully arranged stack of similar images, left on the warehouse floor.

The bodies of Veronica Whitney and Louise Kitan were never recovered. Bloodstains and strands of hair matching their DNA were recovered from the scene along with teeth and fragments of bone leading investigators to believe they were most likely the victims of torture and/or murder.

Chapter Four

October 13th, 2001 - Sydney and Charlie Enter "Doug's Den of Insanity"

Sydney Wuller and Charles Moore were the next two to enter the haunted house. The following is a dramatic retelling of events believed to have occurred, based on photos and evidence found at the scene of their grisly murders.

Sydney and Charlie moved quickly through the three rooms of Doug's Den of Insanity. An awkward silence hung between them, broken only by the occasional creak or recorded scream, until they reached the small albino man waiting at the end of the second room.

"Boo!" he shouted, jumping into position.

"Holy shit, Charlie, a midget!" Sydney shrieked, leaping into his arms.

Charlie shook his head. "Sydney, you can't use that word—it's offensive."

"What?" Sydney looked up at him, eyes wide. "We swear all the time. Since when are you the language police?"

"No, Syd," Charlie said, locking eyes with her, "I mean the word *midget.*"

Sydney's face flushed. "Oh... um. What should I say, then?"

"We prefer *little people,*" the albino man interjected calmly, "or, if you're feeling extra creative, *vertically challenged.* But yeah, he's right—don't call us that."

Sydney's color returned as she climbed down from Charlie's arms, now towering over the haunted house worker. "Maybe I wouldn't have if you hadn't scared the crap out of me."

"Syd," Charlie started disapprovingly, "I don't think it—"

She bopped him on the back of the head. "Don't speak for me."

"Beware the third—" the albino man attempted, only to be cut off.

"No, no, we're not done here," Sydney interrupted.

"Syd, just let him do his job—"

"And what, Charlie? Calm down? Act more like a lady?"

"Hey, *you* cut me off first!" Charlie protested, gesturing wildly.

"So?"

"There's no reason for you to get so... testy with me," Charlie said, his tone sharper.

"Beware the—"

"Hold on a minute!" they both snapped in unison, turning to the small man.

Charlie looked back at Sydney, his eyes softening. "Look, Syd, I think it's awesome that you're tough and don't take crap from anyone, but—"

"Wait..." Sydney blinked, processing his words. "You think I'm awesome?"

Charlie flushed. "Well, yeah... I mean..." He felt his voice trail off. *Come on, you dummy, this is your chance. Just tell her.* He swallowed, clearing his throat. "Syd," he started, voice cracking slightly, "I've always thought you were the coolest, most beautiful, awesome girl I've ever met. I just wish I'd been man enough to tell you sooner—and maybe somewhere better than a haunted house—but you know what? I'm done hiding my feelings. I really like you, Syd. There. I said it."

Sydney held his gaze, standing in silence as Charlie's face turned bright red. *Crap. I said too much,* he thought, feeling his heart pound. *She's embarrassed. Now things are going to be awkward, I'll have to change friend groups... maybe even schools...*

"I..." Sydney reached out, placing a hand on his shoulder. "I like you a lot too, Charlie." She smiled, her cheeks as red as his.

Charlie felt himself melt into his shoes. His face was on fire, but for once, he didn't care. The embarrassment felt not only appropriate but strangely comforting.

"Beware the third and final room!" the albino man announced, stepping forward. "For it—"

"We're having a moment here!" Sydney snapped, turning to glare at him.

The albino man threw his hands up. "You know what? I'm done. Enjoy the rest of the haunted house. I don't get paid enough for this shit." With that, he stalked off, disappearing back into the shadows.

Sydney and Charlie laughed as they entered the third room hand in hand. There was a newfound joy between them as they walked through the eerie, mannequin-lined village, their footsteps almost light.

"Hey, is that Veronica?" Sydney asked, noticing two figures slipping through the door at the other end of the room.

"Yeah, and Louise," Charlie chuckled. "Wonder why it took them so long to finish this kiddie haunted house." He called out, "Hey, guys!" but they vanished through the door without looking back.

"Oh well, we'll catch up to them soon enough," Sydney said, tugging Charlie along as they made their way to the exit. She couldn't help but wonder when Charlie would work up the nerve to kiss her.

Would it be weird to kiss her here? Charlie thought nervously. *Or would she think it's dumb? Having a girlfriend is... complicated.*

Just before they exited into the alley, he turned, took her in his arms, and kissed her. They held each other in a warm embrace, their minds filled with the excitement of new possibilities. Everything felt perfect—until they stopped, and reality set in.

A chorus of screams echoed through the alleyway. Words like *Save Yourself* and *Run* were smeared across the wall opposite them, stark in either spray paint or something darker. Panic gripped them both, and without a word, they bolted toward the warehouse door just as Louise and Veronica had.

Sydney pounded frantically on the door, but it wouldn't budge. "What the hell is going on?"

"Let me try." Charlie nudged her aside and began kicking the door, each impact more desperate as the screams grew deafening, closing in on them. Finally, with one last kick, the door buckled. He forced it open.

"Quick, get inside!" he urged.

She darted through, and he followed, slamming the door shut behind them. For a moment, he watched through the peephole, waiting for whatever horror had chased them to appear. Minutes passed in silence.

"Talk about a hell of an exit, huh?" he chuckled, turning to share a laugh with Sydney. But she didn't respond. The room was empty. "Syd?" he called, his voice rising with concern. *She must've kept running.*

He ventured further into the room, his voice echoing as he called her name. "Syd! Hey, Syd!"

Sydney, meanwhile, had kept running deeper into the warehouse, losing all sense of direction in her panic. Each time she glanced over her shoulder, she saw nothing, but the terror of what might be pursuing her sent chills down her spine. *Oh no, it got him.* She forced herself to keep moving, every nerve on edge, as she imagined the worst for Charlie.

Charlie moved through room after empty room, the warehouse sprawling like a labyrinth, vast and desolate. There were no signs of life—no movement, no sound but his footsteps. With each step, an eerie silence settled around him, amplifying his isolation, and he felt an unsettling loneliness creeping in. He began to miss Sydney's presence more than ever, her absence a gnawing emptiness in the cold dark.

Where could she have gone? He wondered, his thoughts echoing in the hollow stillness. A creeping sensation prickled his skin, a whisper in the back of his mind: *Something's watching you. Someone else is in here.* For a moment, he tried to laugh it off, hoping it was Sydney playing a prank. But the further he ventured, the less he believed it, and a deep, inescapable dread took root.

Sydney's legs burned, and her throat grew hoarse from her frantic breaths. Slowing to a halt, she doubled over, trying to gather herself. *Think, Syd. There has to be a way out.* But she hadn't noticed anything on her desperate sprint into the depths of the warehouse, and now, despite what felt like endless running, she seemed no closer to an exit. The complete silence around her pressed in, amplifying the dread crawling along her skin.

She looked over her shoulder one last time. No trace of Charlie. *He'll catch up. He'll get away from whatever was making that sound, and he'll find me. We'll get out together.* She turned back around—only to walk face-first into a massive spider's web stretching across the room. The sticky threads clung to her, holding her fast in place.

Meanwhile, Charlie continued cautiously through room after room until he stepped into a dimly lit opening. A lone light fixture cast a weak glow over a piece of furniture covered by a white sheet. *That's... strange.* He tried to move around it, but curiosity gnawed at him. *What is it?* His mind whirled, imagining horrors: *What if it's Syd? What if someone hurt her and... hid her there?* His hand trembled as he reached for the sheet, gingerly lifting it.

As the sheet fell away, his heart plummeted. Beneath it was a dentist's chair. *A dentist's chair? What the fu—* He didn't get a chance to finish the thought. A force shoved him forward, and he fell back into the chair.

"Hey, wait!" he screamed, but restraints snaked out, binding his wrists and ankles. Struggling, he looked up to see a man in a white coat, surgical mask in place, adjusting his glasses as he reviewed a clipboard. The overhead light obscured his face.

"Let's see here," the man muttered, flipping through papers. "Charles Moore, age 15... scheduled for a full dental extraction—all thirty-two teeth. Perfect." He pocketed the clipboard and placed a cold metal nose clip on Charlie's face. "Don't worry, I'm a very good dentist," he said with a too-wide smile visible beneath his mask. "And don't worry about nerve blocks. You won't feel a thing—until I'm done."

He stepped aside, revealing a tray laden with tools: pliers, a drill, a dental mirror, gauze, and sutures. Charlie's heart raced.

"For the love of God, no! No!" he screamed as the man approached, pliers gleaming in the dim light.

In another part of the warehouse, Sydney struggled against the thick web. "This isn't real," she whispered, fighting the sticky threads as they tightened around her, pressing into her skin with a strange, stinging numbness. The more she thrashed, the heavier her limbs grew, until she could barely move. As her body went slack, her gaze drifted upward, staring helplessly into the impenetrable darkness above.

It moved slowly at first, savoring the approach to its newly captured prey, but there was no mistaking the gleam in its eight eyes as they peered down from the rafters. A sickening *thump, thump, thump* sounded from above, followed by a deep, sinister hiss as the massive spider descended toward her, crawling along the web with such dizzying speed that Sydney felt her stomach churn.

It came within arm's reach, its breaths heavy and menacing, all eight eyes blinking in unison as it studied her. Her heart hammered, nausea rising as her face grew pale. The spider loomed closer, clicking its segmented legs together, then reared up on its hind legs, spreading its limbs in a display of monstrous size that stole any hope of escape.

Sydney's screams echoed through the merciless darkness, swallowed by the endless, cold silence of its lair.

- All of Charles Moore's teeth, along with fragments of his upper and lower jaw, were recovered from the scene of his disappearance. The first photograph above is believed to have been taken during the removal of his teeth.

- Inside the warehouse, beyond the human remains of the missing teenagers, investigators discovered an enormous spider web. The second image above is a collage of numerous photos of this web, arranged on a single sheet to convey its extensive size.

- It is suspected that Doug [Redacted] captured these photos while Charles Moore was tortured. None of Doug's accomplices—apart from the Ticket Taker—have been found or identified. Authorities believe "Doug's Den of Insanity" has since rebranded and continues touring under a new name, employing heavily disguised personnel. Reports of missing and murdered children associated with this haunted house persist nationwide.

If you have any information regarding this attraction or any relevant details about the case, please contact us at --****.

Chapter Five

October 13th, 2001 - Wes Enters "Doug's Den of Insanity"

*W*es was the last of the teenagers to enter the "Den of Insanity." *He is believed to still be alive.*

Wes moved through Doug's Den of Insanity without a single misstep. Even the little albino man couldn't rattle his steady pace. The first room he found laughable, the second mildly intriguing, and the third felt more like an outdated museum exhibit than a haunted attraction. *Jeez... I feel bad I even suggested this place. I mean, for a dollar, it's not terrible, but they're probably never going to let me live this down.*

As he reached the door leading out from the third room, an icy chill crept down his spine, and he stumbled slightly, his heart suddenly heavy with intense, inexplicable sorrow. He stood, momentarily stunned, as the wave of dread washed over him, rocking him to his core. *What the hell was that?*

Faintly, as if carried on a hidden wind, he heard screams. More unsettling was the eerie familiarity of the voices. *No, it can't be... can it?* Were his friends' voices echoing from somewhere far beyond the Den? He couldn't imagine Doug's Den of Insanity being capable of such horrors. *But what if...?* His stomach twisted as a dark realization sank in—*What if someone out there is doing something horrible to them?*

It struck at the very core of his greatest fear: losing his friends and being powerless to save them. *This was all my idea.* He had always been the one they looked to as a leader.

Without another thought, Wes threw open the door and found himself in a cold, narrow alley. He squinted, his eyes catching crimson letters scrawled across the wall opposite him. *Is... is that blood?* He took a hesitant step forward, his heart pounding as he read the chilling message to himself.

Along the ether, the ephemeral flesh rends,
The forlorn sons drown beneath where light bends,
The shadow strengthens
In Meskatic.
Strange is the night where an alabaster star rises,
And dismal whispers claim the wayward guises,
But stranger still is
Sweet Meskatic.
Songs that shall bring forth ruin,
Where flap the tatters of Vol' Dun,
Must die unheard in
Bleak Meskatic.
Song of my land, my will is spoken,
Die now, left unsung, as tears unspoken

Shall dry and die in
My Lovely Meskatic.

Wes's eyes went wide. *What the hell have we gotten into?* He glanced around, realizing he had exited the building, but with no clear idea where the alleyway led or even which side of the building he was on. A soft rain began to fall, and he watched in horror as the words on the wall slowly dissolved, crimson streaks bleeding down like ink washed away. As they vanished, a low, guttural scream echoed down the alley toward him. Without a second thought, he turned and ran, sprinting down the alley until he stumbled into the yawning darkness of a warehouse.

The door slammed shut behind him, the echo reverberating through the empty building. Wes paused, adjusting his eyes to the dark. Overhead, a faint string of light fixtures stretched out, leading toward what he assumed was the far end of the warehouse. *The madness continues...* He crept forward, straining to listen for any sound of life, but the pounding of his heart was deafening. He could barely keep his nerves steady.

He moved slowly, feeling a wave of nausea and exhaustion grip him. The building itself felt... wrong, as though it had existed in his nightmares long before this night. A strange sensation gnawed at him—*Charlie, Sydney, Louise, Veronica...* he could swear they were close, as if they were somewhere within these same walls, just out of reach. It was impossible to explain, but he felt them, lingering just beyond his senses.

He neared the back door, glancing around the warehouse one last time. The vast, oppressive darkness felt unyielding, making him hesitate. *There's every chance I get lost in here. Or worse... maybe no one else is here.* An idea formed in his mind, and his fear transformed into a sharp resolve. *Doug. I need answers from Doug.*

With newfound determination, he threw open the door and stepped out into the night. The cool air hit him, and he realized how profusely he had been sweating. He found himself standing in an open field that stretched into obscurity on either side. Cautiously, he moved forward, his steps carrying him across what felt like miles of empty space until, finally, he recognized the edge of the parking lot where he had met his friends earlier. He stopped. *Wait a minute... what time is it? How long were we in there?*

The night sky gave him no hint of time's passage, and without a phone or watch, he had no way to gauge how late it had gotten. *I have a feeling we're all going to be in trouble.* It felt like such a juvenile thought given the nightmare he was caught in, but he couldn't shake the hope that maybe, just maybe, the worst thing awaiting him was a lecture from his parents. As he crossed the parking lot toward the small shack where Doug had first greeted them, that hope began to fade.

"Charlie? Veronica? Louise? Syd?" Wes called into the night, his voice tinged with desperation. Only the sound of his footsteps answered him, echoing off the empty lot. His unease grew as he approached the shack, holding his breath as he neared.

The shack was closed, a metal sheet pulled down over the opening where Doug had greeted them. A worn sign that read *Closed* was painted in the same ominous red as the poem he'd seen scrawled on the alley wall. *Well, that's just fuc—*

"Why hello there!" The metal sheet shot up with a crash, and Wes jumped, his heart leaping into his throat.

"Christ!"

"Oh, not even close," Doug replied, leaning forward through the opening, his unsettling grin unchanged. "How are you doing? Wes, wasn't it? Where are the rest of your friends?"

"Don't play dumb." Wes steadied himself, his voice shaking with anger. "Something happened to them. I can feel it in my bones. *You* did something to them."

Doug shrugged, leaning back. "I did no such thing, little buddy. They must not have made it through the Den of Insanity in time." He glanced casually at his wrist. "Looks like they've got about ten minutes left to make it out, as per our agreement."

"Or else what?" Wes demanded, staring him down, feeling the cold twist of dread tighten in his gut.

Doug's grin widened. "They'll meet a terrible fate... if they haven't already."

"What the hell is going on?" Wes demanded, his voice taut with anger and fear.

"Well, remember those little tickets you and your friends turned in before entering the Den? You see, I thought it would make things more... immersive to incorporate some of your fears into the experience."

"What does that even mean?" Wes's stomach churned.

"That big old warehouse I use for storage out back... after the first round of scares—the ones meant for kids—I decided to repurpose it for something a little more... tailored for older guests." Doug patted himself on the back. "Each of you has a unique experience set up, customized just for you."

Wes's eyes narrowed. "I didn't see anything in that warehouse. What's happening to them in there?"

Doug rummaged through his pocket, pulling out scraps of paper. He thumbed through them as if skimming a grocery list. "Let's see... Louise, life-like mannequins. She's probably dealing with some of the residents of that quaint little European village from room three. Veronica? Darkness and isolation—I'd wager she's trapped somewhere, no light, no way out. Charles..." Doug chuckled. "Classic. He's getting his teeth extracted by a particularly sadistic dental 'specialist.' And Sydney? Typical arachnophobia. She's probably meeting up with Gouse, my very large, well-fed spider. Nice lady."

Wes stared in disbelief. "Where the hell did you find a giant spider?"

"Same place I found living mannequins and a sadistic oral surgeon. And Ernie, too. There was a sale going on."

"Ernie?"

"Yeah," Doug frowned, as if surprised. "The albino guy who works in room two. You saw him, right?"

"Yes, I know who you're talking about, but—"

"Good, good, no offense, but you never know with union workers," Doug sighed. "Especially that damned Local 652 and ½. Sure, I get that they're particular, but *do* they really need the '½'? It feels a bit dramatic, don't you think? We get it, you're all little people," he shrugged, then looked back at the papers.

"And last but not least," he continued, "Wes... fear of losing his friends." Doug glanced up, smirking. "Well, looks like you've lost them all." He laughed, a deep, gleeful sound as if he'd just delivered the best punchline in the world.

"No. No, there wasn't any of that in the warehouse. You're making this up—you couldn't—"

Doug cracked his knuckles, a satisfied gleam in his eyes. "That warehouse is special, kid. It doesn't follow what you'd call linear time or traditional dimensions." He pointed back over his shoulder. "It was a gift from an old friend."

"What the fuck does that even mean? Who did you get it from?" Wes demanded, still struggling to grasp the situation.

Doug leaned in, smiling darkly. "Like I said, an old friend. The same one who wrote that poem in the alleyway. Although I doubt you-"

"That weird-ass poem? About Meska, whatever?" Wes clenched his fists, barely holding back his rage.

Doug's expression turned reverent. "You... you saw *The History of Meskatic*?" His voice dropped as if it were a sacred subject.

Wes slammed his fist on the counter. "Does that even matter right now?"

Doug straightened, regaining his composure. "I suppose not. But it's a rare honor to see the history of Meskatic. My friend doesn't let just anyone in on that. You should feel privileged."

"Are you even listening to me, asshole?" Wes's body shook with fury.

Doug waved a hand. "Yeah, yeah, kiddo, I hear you. But listen—I may have an idea on how to save your friends' souls."

Wes took a step back, feeling his stomach drop. "Their *souls?*"

Doug sighed loudly as if the answer were obvious. "Here's the deal, man. If you agree to come work for me, I'll let them all go. Seems fair, right? Four lives for one—it's a bargain. Besides," he added with a knowing smirk, "it's pretty clear he wants *you*."

Wes felt completely powerless. He had no idea how to save his friends, no plan, no recourse—except for this twisted offer. *You brought them here. You owe it to them. They didn't even want to come.* He clenched his fists. "What exactly does working for you entail?"

"Well, you'd be working for the big boss—just like I do. I serve our dark lord, Vol'... well, you know what, that's not important. Great guy, though. Anyways, you'd be my new ticket taker at the entrance to the Den of Insanity. You'd collect those little slips of paper with people's fears and bring them back to the shack. That's it. Not glamorous, but necessary. My current ticket taker's kind of a bum and, between us," Doug leaned in conspiratorially, "I don't like his musical tastes."

Wes's mind raced. "You'll let my friends go... if I take this job?"

"Yes. And to be transparent, come daylight, the Den of Insanity moves on. So I need your decision *now*. And I'll be honest, you won't get to say goodbye, you won't come back to this town, and you'll never see the friends you saved again. But hey, clear conscience, right?"

Wes took a deep, shuddering breath. *You can't leave them to suffer. How could you live with yourself if you do?*

"You promise you'll let them go free?"

"Just as I said, Wes." Doug's face turned solemn. "I'll release their souls. In exchange, I get *you*." He dusted off his shoulders, extending a hand. "So, we shake on it. What do you say?"

- The following picture is believed to be the remains of either one of the mannequins or perhaps a person midway transformation into one of the living mannequins Doug kept in the "European Village".

- The rest are believed to have been burned inside the incinerator found back behind the warehouse.

Chapter Six

October 13th, 2001 - Wes Makes a Deal with Doug, the Proprietor of "Doug's Den of Insanity"

*T*he following account is a reconstruction of the exchange between Wes Andrews and the entity known as "Doug," pieced together from available evidence and testimony. This description reflects the closest approximation of events following their fateful arrangement.

At first, warmth spread through Wes's hand as he gripped Doug's, but within moments, it turned bitterly cold, then numb, until he felt nothing at all. Doug's iron grip held firm and the gleam in his eyes removed any lingering doubt: Wes had sealed his fate. Wes drew in a sharp breath, feeling a stabbing chill lodge deep within his lungs, filling him with pain so intense he doubled over, coughing without relief.

"There, there, buddy boy," Doug chuckled, his voice dripping with satisfaction. "I see you're already feeling the effects of joining the workforce. They call it work, after all, not play."

"My... my friends..." Wes forced the words out through gritted teeth. "You... promised."

Doug released his hand, giving a theatrical bow. "Of course. I'm a man of my word." He stepped aside, gesturing to a small television screen mounted on the wall. "They'll be set free, one by one. You can watch to make sure there's no funny business."

Through blurred vision, Wes strained to make out the image on the screen. The wavy brown hair, the rounded face—"L... Louise?"

A loud slap jolted him, and he turned to see Doug's arm draped casually over his shoulder. "Indeed! Can you believe she's terrified of mannequins? How delightfully childish!" Doug laughed, slapping Wes on the shoulder so hard it nearly knocked him down. "She'll be the first soul I release. You should watch—it's going to be rather... interesting." Doug dug through his jacket pockets and pulled them inside out. "Damn, wish I had some popcorn."

"Don't hurt her... please..." Wes gasped, dizzy with pain and unable to close his eyes, his body locked in place.

"Oh, I'm not hurting her, kiddo," Doug's grip on Wes's shoulder tightened, cold as iron. "But I can't guarantee what the residents of that little European village might do to her before she... passes."

"*Passes?*" Wes tried to scream, but his voice cracked. "You promised!"

"I promised to let their souls go," Doug said, his voice almost mocking. "And I intend to keep that promise. I won't trap them in the Den for my lord and savior. But I never said I'd let them live, did I? You didn't ask for that."

"You *bastard!*" With a final surge of strength, Wes swung a fist, connecting with the bridge of Doug's nose. Blood splattered back on him, burning his skin like acid. Wes fell to his knees, vision blurring as the pain seared through his face and chest.

Doug sighed, pulling a handkerchief from his pocket to dab at his nose. "Oh, Wes, I really wish you hadn't done that. You're *really* not going to like what happens next."

"Fu...ck... you..." Wes wheezed, his defiance fading. His eyes glazed over with a thick, black sheen, his entire body shuddering as an icy numbness spread to his core.

"Wessss..." A low voice grumbled from the void, curling into his mind. "You will now see... the purpose all must ssserve. What all of us desire... the salvation I bring to your kind, as I have to countless others before. Look. Gaze upon my majesty and marvel at the greatnesss yet to come."

Darkness gave way, and Wes found himself kneeling on coarse sand. Blinding heat bore down from above, and he squinted, staring up into a blackened sphere hanging low in the sky. He looked around—a barren desert stretched to the horizon, sand tinted a sickly crimson.

Pale, misshapen clouds hung above him. They looked like massive sheets of flesh, grotesquely stitched together, drifting across the sky. Faces left intact, stared down at him with hollow, screaming mouths, their wails filling the air, eerily familiar. *They were once people,* he realized, their lives twisted into these terrible forms.

"Meskatic... home... paradise..." the voice growled in his mind.

The wind bit into his skin like icy needles, and he looked down, noticing the crimson sands more closely. *Blood,* he thought, realizing the ground was scattered with bones, shattered fragments of countless lives ground into dust. It flowed with the wind, scouring him with each gust.

"Their monumentsss... their defiance and their bones... turned to dust, to blow along a merciless wind. All who challenge Vol' Dun are dessstroyed. Turn... and face me."

The voice scraped against Wes's mind like stone grinding on bone. He clenched his hands to his ears, burying his head in the sand to block out the words, but the voice only grew louder.

"*Face me, boy!*"

Wes felt his chest cave in as claws wrapped around him, plucking him from the sand. He opened his eyes, screaming as he was lifted toward Vol' Dun. The creature loomed above him, its twenty-seven eyes glistening with malice, its crooked mouth curling into a twisted smile. It stood fully erect, leathery wings spreading wide, their ominous hum vibrating through Wes's bones with a promise of nothing but oblivion and pain. Most horrific of all was Vol' Dun's smile, each tooth a jagged, uneven razor, their stench unbearable. Wes vomited over the claws holding him like a ragdoll.

"Pretty, isn't it?"

Wes blinked, and the nightmare vanished. He found himself staring into Doug's gray eyes, the numbness evaporating and replaced by a sickening dread.

"You look like hell, kid." Doug reached down and hauled Wes to his feet, glancing at his vomit-streaked clothes. "But hey, welcome to the team." He slipped a "Doug's Den of Insanity" T-shirt over Wes's head. "Used to sell these in the gift shop, back when we had one.

Too many shoplifters though." Doug lowered his voice. "But enough about that." He gestured toward the shack. "Time to get this show on the road."

Wes stumbled, mouth agape as his eyes focused on a small monitor in the corner, displaying a scene inside the warehouse. *Louise.*

"Get away from me, you fucking creeps!" Louise shrieked, backing into a corner. Pale, blank faces surrounded her, staring with lifeless eyes as they shuffled closer, their rigid movements both unnatural and grotesque. She clutched her chest, her breaths coming shallow and fast as fear overtook her.

"It doesn't hurt," a disembodied voice floated above the ambling figures. "Once you become one of us... nothing hurts anymore."

"No! Get away!" Louise swung her arm, knocking the head off one of the child-sized mannequins.

"*Jimmy!*" the figures roared in unison. "We protect our own, Louise. We won't stand for this violence."

Louise felt the cold wall pressing against her as sweat poured down her back. Her lungs seemed to shrink, each breath weaker than the last. She slid to her knees, clutching her chest. "Just... leave me alone," she whispered, curling into herself. "Veronica... where are you?" Her voice was barely audible.

"Get her... kill her..." the voice commanded as the figures moved in, closer and closer.

Louise's left arm spasmed with a sudden pain, her hand pressing desperately over her heart. Her vision blurred as her breathing became shallow, her limbs growing limp. She collapsed to the floor, curling up in a final act of self-preservation. Cold, lifeless limbs closed in, and everything went black.

The screen on the monitor filled with mannequins, smothering her as the display faded to darkness. Wes stood frozen, unable to move, his mind reeling. Doug nodded, his expression unbothered.

"Tsk, tsk, tsk shame about your friend," Doug said, tapping Wes on the shoulder. "But don't worry." He flashed a grin. "She won't be turned into one of them."

"L-Louise..." Wes's voice cracked, tears stinging his eyes.

"Oh, she'll be torn apart and rebuilt in plastic," Doug laughed, the sound grating. "Just like one of those, what do you call 'em? Mold-a-somethings?"

"Bastard..." Wes choked back his tears, barely able to stand under the weight of grief and horror.

Doug gave an approving nod. "One down." He turned to the monitor. "She went in with Veronica, didn't she? Let's check in on her next." Doug's grin reflected in the blank screen as it flickered and focused on Veronica, standing alone in the pitch-black warehouse. "Didn't even need anything special for her. Just the dark. Honestly? Lamer than Louise, I have to say."

"Don't..." Wes whispered, his voice faint as his strength drained away. His mouth felt dry and tasted of dust, his legs as heavy as stone, rooting him to the spot.

"Hmm... yeah, it could take a while for her to die in there. Starvation, dehydration, the whole works." Doug shrugged. "But we need to be out by sunrise, so I think I'll speed things up." He closed his eyes, muttering a few words Wes couldn't understand. "There we go. Now we just sit back and watch."

Veronica sat in the middle of the empty warehouse, knees pulled to her chest, rocking back and forth. *They'll come for you. Someone will come for you.* It was the only thought anchoring her sanity, her final comfort against the creeping darkness.

A sudden skidding sound broke the silence, making her jolt to her feet.

"Who's there?" She squinted into the void, her mind conjuring silhouettes. "Louise? Syd? Charlie? Wes?" But only the pounding of her heartbeat answered her. The stillness pressed in, haunting her. *There's nothing there. You're hearing things. Seeing things.*

She coughed, the sound echoing strangely, as though from miles away. *That's... strange.* Her vision started to dim. *What's happening?* Her legs wobbled, and a heavy exhaustion swept over her. *Am I... fainting?*

She lowered herself to sit, but her legs buckled beneath her. Pain flared as her wrists gave way, snapping as she collapsed face-first onto the floor. *What the...* She fought against the agony, struggling to move, but her strength was gone. She opened her mouth to scream, and her teeth scattered onto the floor, clattering in the silent void. The last thing she saw was the warehouse around her, dark and empty, as her body gave in—her lungs deflated, her brain shriveled, and her heart slowed until it finally stopped.

"There. Now she doesn't have to suffer a prolonged death," Doug murmured, releasing Wes's shoulder. He turned back toward his booth, disappearing behind the counter for a moment. After a clattering of metal, he emerged, carrying a folding chair. "These old bones don't hold up like they used to." He unfolded the chair beside Wes, settling in with a sigh. "We're halfway through. This would be the perfect time for a bathroom break, but"—he pointed at Wes's soaked jeans—"I doubt you've got anything left."

His piercing laugh rang out, nearly snapping Wes out of his stupor. But Wes's mind was fried from the horrors he had just witnessed.

Doug rummaged through his trouser pocket and pulled out a shiny quarter. "Heads, we check in with Sydney. Tails, we take a peek at little

Charlie." He flipped the coin, and Wes watched, heart pounding, as it arced in slow motion, reaching its apex before plummeting back down to Doug's hand. He slapped it onto his forearm, locking eyes with Wes.

"Don't worry, kiddo. They're both dead either way. This is just to decide who goes first." He uncovered the coin. "Tails. Mr. Charles Moore it is." The blank monitor flickered to life, revealing a sparse, empty warehouse. This time, however, a lone dentist's chair stood at the center, and strapped to it, writhing in agony, was Charlie.

"Now, now, Mr. Moore, we're almost done here," the figure in blue scrubs cooed, his once-white gloves stained crimson, the goggles over his eyes splattered with blood. The dentist gave Charlie a cold smile, bending over the chair.

Charlie struggled, barely able to comprehend the agony flooding his senses. *Just let me die. Please... let me die.* His blue eyes were vacant, holding only a hollow, ineffable pain. His mouth throbbed, his head pounded, each heartbeat sending fresh waves of torment through his body. Nearly all his teeth had been removed—he could see them glistening on a metal tray beside him, a ghastly collection of his own extracted bones.

"We're down to the third and fourth molars on the right and left," the dentist noted, checking his clipboard. "Won't take more than ten minutes, Charles. Then you'll get a toy from the chest, and I'll have my receptionist give you the bill."

The dentist pressed the bite block into the back of Charlie's mouth, forcing it open despite his resistance. "Hope you have insurance." He chuckled, watching as Charlie's tears mingled with the blood pooling in his mouth. "Here we go." With a casual twist, he clamped down on Charlie's last molar with cold forceps and pulled. Charlie's scream was muffled by the bite block, his tongue pressing desperately against it as he tried to shift his head away.

"Now, now, keep that tongue still, or I might have to extract it as well."

Charlie, trembling, tucked his tongue away in terror, knowing he couldn't withstand anymore. He convulsed, sobbing uncontrollably as his spirit broke. *I'm going to die here. Alone. A virgin...* The thought of Sydney's face flickered in his mind, a bittersweet memory that filled him with longing, momentarily numbing the agony.

But only for a moment. The dentist gave a final yank, pulling out the tooth, and Charlie's vision blurred, his head lolling as waves of dizziness overtook him. Glancing down at the bloody tarp beneath him, he saw the dark stains spreading around him. *So much blood...*

A surge of nausea hit him as he rocked back in the seat. *Please... not like this. I don't want to die like this. For the love of God, leave me some dignity.*

Charlie heaved, but the bite block trapped the flow of vomit in his mouth, mingling with the coagulated blood and forcing him to retch harder. His stomach acid burned the raw holes where his teeth once proudly sat, the searing pain nearly unbearable. Thrashing his head back against the headrest, he tried desperately to free himself from the restraints, twisting his neck back and forth with futile force. Finally, he choked, and the vomit spewed from his nose, splattering over the tarp below.

His vision blurred as he struggled for breath, a viscous mixture gathering in his throat, trapping him in a breathless chokehold. His eyes rolled back as he succumbed to the darkness. *Syd... I'm so sorry... I wish I'd said something sooner...* In his final moments, Charles Moore thought only of the things he would never do and the people he would never see again. Death claimed him before the dentist could finish extracting his last tooth.

The dentist stood over him, removing his mask and gloves with an air of calm disappointment. "What a shame." He pocketed each bloodied tooth from the tray, casting a last glance over Charlie's body. "Now I'll need to find someone else to complete the set for those dentures I'd been meaning to make." The dentist removed his gloves and with a resigned sigh, he turned and faded into the dark recesses of the warehouse, leaving Charlie's blood-soaked body slumped in the chair. The monitor flickered, then went black.

Doug's grin widened as he turned to Wes. "I hate dentists, don't you?"

Wes felt his stomach plummet, sinking into a hollow freefall of horror. "Charlie... I..."

"He can't hear you, silly," Doug chuckled, his voice dripping with mock sympathy. "He's dead."

Wes toppled forward, curling into the fetal position on the cold cement.

Doug bent down, hauling Wes up and setting him in the folding chair. "Hey, now," he dusted him off, gripping his shoulders, "there's only one of your friends left now. Sydney, wasn't it?" Doug examined Wes's blank expression, the dimming light in his eyes. *I must've broken him,* he thought, stifling a sigh. *Well, that's no fun.* He leaned closer, staring into the empty, dark pools of Wes's eyes. *Perfect for my operation,* he mused. *Once his soul is completely gone.*

Doug's own gaze drifted as he recalled his younger days, the first glimmer of ambition he'd had as a fresh dropout from college, eager to build "the biggest and baddest haunted house in the Midwest." It had been his dream since his first visit to the haunted barn at the local pumpkin farm. And then they'd come—what he thought were merely traveling evangelists. They'd seemed cold, and hungry, so he'd invited them inside. They spoke of their lord and savior, Vol' Dun. Before he understood what was happening, they'd pinned him down, drawing their own blood to anoint his face, pouring it into his mouth, forcing him to drink. Then came the whispers. At first quiet, small disruptions throughout his day, then inescapable screams that commanded his very existence.

The evangelists vanished, leaving him curled and broken on the floor, a new disciple of Vol' Dun, god of darkness and despair. "Doug's Haunted House" had transformed overnight into "Doug's Den of Insanity," no longer just a spectacle of cheap thrills. It was now a traveling temple of worship, bringing unsuspecting souls under Vol' Dun's gaze—some directly, others, like Wes and his friends, in far more torturous, circuitous ways. And it wouldn't end with them; others from their town had already felt Vol' Dun's influence without realizing it. As the whispers spread with the dawn, they would seek new places to congregate, drawing others into Vol' Dun's growing fold.

Doug stared into Wes's empty eyes for a long moment, satisfied, before turning his attention to the blank monitor. "One more matter of business," he murmured, straightening and bowing his head as he gestured to the screen. "Gouse, show us why you're the most revered spider of our congregation." The screen flickered on and off, and Wes prayed with every fiber of his being that it would remain unfocused and dark, but a paralyzing chill swept over him, locking his body in place as he felt his last shred of free will slip away.

"If this is some kind of fucking joke, I'm going to sue *all* of you!" Sydney spat, thrashing against the sticky, silken threads that held her fast. Her struggling undulated the entire web, but she couldn't look away from the eight unblinking eyes descending toward her. The spider's legs moved with a terrifying slither across the webs, a sound that echoed hollowly in the silent warehouse. She knew, deep down, there was no one around.

If I can just get my hand free. She still had one last ace up her sleeve.

Her parents' words echoed in her mind: "It's nothing too crazy, and we don't want you showing it off, but we think a girl your age might need this." They'd presented her with a fold-up knife—six inches in length, with a serrated backside and a tiny compass embedded in the hilt.

"God forbid you ever need to cut through some kind of restraints," her mother had said, her voice tense. "The very thought makes me sick, but your father's right. Better to have it and not need it than the other way around."

Her father had placed a reassuring hand on her shoulder. "I trust you, Syd. Use it only if you absolutely must," he'd said, folding her hand over the knife. "And I really hope that day never comes." Since that night, she'd kept it tucked away, always ready—just in case.

Now, as Sydney struggled, she could feel her feet barely touching the cold cement, but the thick webbing held her firmly, an inescapable embrace around her torso and arms. She tilted her head up, forced to watch as her captor descended, fluid dripping from its gaping maw. Its oversized fangs clacked rhythmically, mimicking chewing, preparing to devour her whole. *Either this monster of a spider or me. One of us is walking away.*

Desperation formed an idea in her mind. *Hell, what do I have to lose?* She reversed direction, twisting into the web. With each turn, the sticky threads stretched, pulling her closer to the ground.

Gouse loomed closer, each step more menacing, until she felt its rancid breath on her face. She went limp and dropped to the floor just as the spider lunged, flying past her and crashing head-first into the cement. *Now's my chance.* Rolling onto her side, Sydney pressed the webbing against the serrated bristles on the spider's leg, frantically sawing back and forth. *Come on, come on!* The web snapped, and her hand shot down to her pocket, pulling out the knife. She flipped it open, its size pitifully small in comparison to the beast before her.

No time for fear now, Syd. Live or die. She took a step back, held the knife aloft, and leaped, screaming as she plunged the blade into the spider's thorax. Gouse shrieked, whirling around in confusion, but she held on, the knife twisting in her white-knuckled grip as she clung to its back. Hoisting herself onto its body, she yanked the blade out and drove it in again and again.

"Why won't you fucking die!" she screamed, her voice barely audible over the spider's wails. Gouse staggered, skittering frantically around the room, but she held fast, refusing to let go. The creature's deafening roar shook the walls as it bucked, trying to dislodge her.

"It's just you and me!" Sydney shouted, her voice wild with adrenaline. She slit open the spider's back and dug her hands inside, tearing and ripping at the soft flesh within. Warm, viscous fluids coated her arms, sticky and rank, as she kept slicing. Finally, her strength gave out, and she tumbled off the spider, rolling across the ground. The creature turned, its eight eyes narrowing as it stared her down. Sydney pushed herself up, raising her knife as she crouched, ready for the final attack.

Gouse charged. Sydney sprinted toward it, knife raised high. Leaping into the air, she held the blade with both hands, aiming straight down. The spider lifted its fangs, grabbing her mid-air and biting into her ribs. She cried out in agony, feeling the sharp fangs dig into her flesh, but with a final surge of strength, she plunged the knife into Gouse's skull, twisting until the spider went limp, releasing her.

She fell to the ground beside the carcass, blood pooling around her. A smirk crossed her face as her vision dimmed. "Got you, asshole," she whispered, her eyes closing as she bled out next to the massive monster she had slain. The monitor flickered, then faded to black.

Doug kicked the folding chair out from beneath Wes, cursing as he watched the scene end. "Dammit!" He picked up the chair and hurled it across the parking lot. "There's no fucking time for cleaning up this mess!"

Wes lay crumpled on the cold ground, feeling every ounce of strength leave him. *Just stay here, let yourself rot. It's what you deserve.* The thought lingered, comforting in its finality until it was wrenched from him.

Do as Doug commands. You belong to us now. Obey my prophet's orders. The voice of Vol' Dun echoed within him, powerful and undeniable. Wes shook his head, trying to rid himself of the intrusion, but it was futile. His body and mind were no longer his own.

- This is the incinerator located directly behind the aforementioned warehouse.

- Remains of four of the five missing children were found within it as well as numerous other missing persons, haunted house props, and other items.

- It is believed to be one of potentially many utilized by Doug to keep evidence left behind at a minimum.

Chapter Seven

October 13th, 2001 - Midnight

"On your feet, kiddo," Doug barked, snapping Wes out of his stupor. Wes staggered upright, his movements robotic, and followed as Doug gestured for him to move. "That's better," Doug grinned. "Now come with me. We've got a warehouse to clean and a lot to pack up."

Suddenly, the parking lot was filled with people—almost the entire town, shuffling in eerie silence. Doug's commands echoed as they drifted like puppets into the Den of Insanity. Together, they dismantled the haunted house, carefully packing each prop into boxes, and loading them into a large unmarked truck. Behind the wheel, the little albino man honked periodically. "Hurry it up, flesh bags! I'm on the clock here. If I have to explain to the union why I worked overtime again, I'm blaming all of you!"

As the last props were stowed away, the townsfolk filed silently into the back of the truck, destined to travel with their new "temple" and worship Vol' Dun whenever he demanded. They worked tirelessly through the night, and by dawn, they were mopping up Gouse's remains from the warehouse floor. Doug checked his wrist, then yelled, "Damn it! No time for the web. Just leave it. Everyone into the truck! We're moving!"

Wes stepped toward the truck bed, ready to climb in, but Doug blocked him. "Not you, Wes. You're riding up front with me. We've got a lot to talk about." Doug's face twisted into a devilish grin, his teeth glinting in the early sunlight. "I've got big plans for us, kiddo." Together, they climbed into Doug's rusted baby blue sedan. Doug adjusted the rearview mirror and started the engine.

As the car lumbered along the town's edge, Wes caught a final glimpse of his childhood home fading into the distance. A tear escaped down his cheek as he sat paralyzed, helpless to change his fate. *It's all my fault*. The weight of grief and guilt pressed into his chest, the full horror of his situation settling in.

Doug took a long drag from a cigarette, exhaling smoke into the confined space without rolling down the window. "Take a good look, Wes," he sneered. "We're never coming back to this dump." His laughter filled the car as Wes stared out the window, watching his world disappear on the horizon. Images of his parents, the bodies of his friends, and the life he'd left behind drifted through his mind, becoming as distant as the town vanishing behind them. *Never again*.

Doug exhaled another plume of smoke. "One day, I'll need someone to take over this whole operation, you know?" He glanced at Wes, his smile wicked. "There's a lot I'm going to need to teach you in case something happens to me. But just promise me one thing." His smile widened. "Promise you won't change the name to 'Wes's Den of Insanity.'" He slapped Wes's knee, howling with laughter. "But seriously, I wouldn't appreciate that. Not after bringing you into this brand-new world."

Wes swallowed hard, his throat barely able to release a single word. "Where?" His voice was hoarse, but the question had clawed its way out. Leaving everything behind was terrifying, and the only way to ease that fear was to know, at least, where they were headed.

Doug yawned, the rising sun casting an eerie glow through the smoke-filled car. "Not sure yet," he answered, squinting against the brightness of the morning. The cheerful light outside mocked Wes's inner torment. "I wait for the boss to tell me where we're headed exactly. We've got to make sure we don't run into any other, ah, obstacles along the way. All I know is we're headed west. Maybe the coast, maybe Oregon. Doesn't matter. I believe in Vol' Dun, and Vol' Dun favors me."

Smoke clouded Wes's lungs, stinging his eyes. His tears flowed freely now, and he made no effort to hide them. Waves of grief crashed over him, mingling with a new, sharper feeling—rage. He raised a trembling hand to wipe his face and felt something different spark within him. *He can't know.* For a fleeting moment, he allowed himself a slight smile. His recent discovery brought a surge of clarity and something else: purpose.

As he thought of Charlie, Sydney, Veronica, and Louise, a single word echoed in his mind: revenge. His hands balled into fists as he glanced sideways at Doug, the images of needles, knives, and fire flooding his mind. *I could take the wheel. Crash us both into a tree.* But the thought didn't satisfy him. *No. He needs to suffer.* Wes began to visualize countless ways to exact his vengeance, each more painful than the last. *And I have all the time in the world now.*

Slumping back in his seat, Wes forced himself to appear broken, resigned—a mindless servant. *Play along. Make him believe.* He would bide his time until Doug let down his guard. The Den of Insanity would serve its purpose, a means to gather everything Wes needed to execute his plan.

As the car merged onto the interstate, Wes cast a sidelong glance at Doug, who stared off into the distance, lost in his own twisted thoughts. The smoke-laden car cruised along in silence. Wes unclenched his fists, the tension ebbing into a sense of dark satisfaction. *One day, Doug*, he thought, closing his eyes and allowing his mind to drift into that cold resolve. *One day soon... you'll be mine.*

Until next year, kiddos.

With love,

Doug

Made in the USA
Columbia, SC
06 March 2025

54738352R00043